The Richest Doll in the World

POLLY M. ROBERTUS

HOLIDAY HOUSE • NEW YORK

First Edition
1 3 5 7 9 10 8 6 4 2

Library of Congress Cataloging-in-Publication Data

Robertus, Polly M.
The richest doll in the world / by Polly Robertus. — 1st ed.
p. cm.
Summary: The Christmas after her parents' death,
Emily wants no gift but to see the wonderful doll of
her grandmother's employer, Mrs. Bigley, but the old
woman, who has also experienced a terrible loss, will not
allow a child near her treasured heirloom.
ISBN 978-0-8234-2121-3 (hardcover)
[1. Dolls—Fiction.   2. Old age—Fiction.   3. Wealth—
Fiction.   4. Dogs—Fiction.   5. Grief—Fiction.
6. Orphans—Fiction.   7. Christmas—Fiction.]   I. Title.
PZ7. R5515Ric 2008
[Fic]—dc22
2007035466

To Carole, Cynthia, Jean, Lynn, Sean,
and especially Jon—
without you,
this book would not have happened.

And to "Ann," who got safely home

Contents

The Richest Doll in the World

CHAPTER *1*

"The Worst Christmas Ever . . ."

"**W**HY won't you believe me, Grandma Rose?" Emily scolded. "I don't want anything for Christmas. I just want to see that doll. Take me with you! Don't make me go to day care on Christmas Eve."

Her grandmother put down the brush she had just used on Emily's thick, dark hair. "For the last time," she said firmly, beginning to braid. "You're going to Mrs. Debbs's and that's all there is to it. I've told you a thousand times that Mrs. Bigley won't let anyone but herself and me near that doll. The one time I asked her if you could come, she got so upset I thought I would lose my job. A fine Christmas *that* would make!" She fastened an elastic band at the bottom of one braid and began the next.

"But—"

"No *buts*! And please hold still. You and I will have a wonderful Christmas Eve starting tonight, and tomorrow will be Christmas. I know you'll like your presents."

Emily folded her arms across her chest and scowled at her grandmother in the mirror. Her voice went flat. "I already *said* I don't want any presents. I just want to see that—"

Grandma Rose squeezed Emily's shoulders and gave her a tiny shake. "Emily, honey . . ." They looked into the mirror at each other, at Grandma Rose's sad face and Emily's set, unsmiling one. "This is the hardest Christmas either of us will ever have, sweetheart. *Ever.* We have to help each other through it. Your mother and daddy wouldn't want us to go on being sad forever, any more than they wanted to be in that crash last summer. And they especially wouldn't want us to be unhappy at Christmastime." She gave Emily a kiss on top of her head. "Now, let's make the best of it we can. It's what *they* would want."

Emily, who had gone stiff at the mention of her parents, glared. "I still don't want presents. All I want, in the whole, wide world—"

"*Emily!*" Grandma Rose went back to the second braid. "I've told you and told you! It's not just that Mrs. Bigley pays me so well to be her housekeeper—goodness knows I couldn't make enough anywhere else to keep us going—but that doll is not a toy to her. Not at all. It means much more to her than you or I can understand. Mrs. Bigley is old and sad and . . . probably a little crazy. She always gets even more peculiar at Christmastime and she's been frantic lately. If I didn't go in to work today, I don't know what would happen to her. *She* needs me, too, Emily."

Emily's scowl faded. She looked up at her

grandmother's face in the mirror. "But why is she crazy? What happened to her?"

"Oh, honey, I don't know. She's so full of secrets. All I know is, she's lived in that creepy old place all alone for years and years. She must have had feelings for human beings once, but now . . . Everything she should feel for other people goes toward that doll."

Emily stayed quiet, thinking.

"Is Santa Claus going to come to the doll, too?"

Grandma Rose finished the braid. "Mrs. Bigley is certainly pretending that he will! She's so worried, though—she's been looking for weeks and hasn't found the right present yet. Whatever that might be!" She kissed Emily again. "Now, we're already running late, and the radio said something just a while ago about the weather getting really, really bad. The sooner I get to work, the sooner I'll be done and we can start our Christmas. Scoot! Get your coat on."

"If I can't come with you, *why* can't I just stay here? I'm old enough."

"EMILY!" Grandma Rose's voice mixed frustration and sorrow in a way that finally silenced her granddaughter. Emily found her coat and hat and pulled them on.

"Mittens and muffler and boots, too!" Grandma Rose called. "We're getting a storm, by the sound of that wind."

They met at the door. "I wish we could leave the Christmas tree lights on," Grandma Rose said fondly, fumbling through her purse for her keys. "It would look so nice to come home to." Reluctantly, she turned the lights off. "Okay, here we go!"

CHAPTER 2

Emily's Drastic Decision

Grandma Rose pulled open the door, and she and Emily stepped out of the tiny house. A fierce wind brought tears to their eyes and made them pull their mufflers over their faces. They couldn't talk, but walked as fast as they could, the wind shoving them into each other. When they turned the corner, the wind began to thrust itself at their backs and Emily had to grab on to her grandmother's coat.

As they walked toward her day care center, Emily began to daydream about Mrs. Bigley's doll. *Delilah*. The name sounded almost magical. It sounded like "delightful." But the doll's name was just the beginning of everything that fascinated Emily about her.

Delilah must be the richest doll in the world, Emily thought. Richer people than Mrs. Bigley might own special dolls, but they probably had lots of dolls. Mrs. Bigley had just one. But *that* doll . . .

When Emily had moved in with her, Grandma Rose, to comfort her, had told her stories about her odd employer and her antique doll. Mrs. Bigley lived alone in an enormous, dark, stone house. The house sat at the center of a park enclosed by a spiky, iron fence. It had a real tower and many chimneys. Mrs. Bigley had once been very rich, with a house full of servants. But over many years she had sold off possessions, closed one room after another, and fired the help. Now she lived in just a couple of rooms near the top of the house. No one else but Grandma Rose had been inside for a long time.

"Does she live in the tower?" Emily had asked. How thrilling to live in a tower!

"No. I've never been in the tower, but it's near the rooms Mrs. Bigley still uses. They're up at the top of one side of the house. The tower is at the very corner. There used to be another tower at the other end of the house, but it's fallen down now."

From what Grandma Rose said, Emily came to understand that Delilah the doll "lived" in a sort of apartment near the tower. Mrs. Bigley had a few pieces of her own furniture, a tiny bedroom, a closert, a kitchen, and bathroom there, but all the rest of the space—two big rooms with a corridor connecting them—really belonged to Delilah.

Grandma Rose felt Mrs. Bigley might have spent most of her fortune buying treasures for Delilah. She had sold off the contents of one room of the mansion after another partly to pay taxes and expenses, but mostly to buy things for the doll. Meanwhile, the rest of the house gradually went to ruin.

Emily had begged to see the doll since the first time she'd heard about it, but Grandma Rose always refused. And at every no, Emily's curiosity increased.

Grandma Rose and Emily turned another corner, and the wind went mad around them, pushing from all directions at once. Grandma Rose grabbed Emily's hand, as if she feared the wind would blow her away, but Emily hardly noticed. She went right on thinking about that empty old house.

"Is the tower empty, too?" Emily had asked. The idea of the tower thrilled her.

"There must be something in there," Grandma Rose said. "The door that leads to it is locked, though, and I've never been through it. But Mrs. Bigley takes a dust cloth in there sometimes, and she just disappears through the door for an hour or two and locks it behind her."

Emily wondered what could be behind that

door, as they got near the little, beat-up house where she usually went after school.

The sight of it shattered her daydreams. Grandma Rose opened the gate and gave her a hug that Emily barely noticed. Emily turned away and dragged up the sidewalk. She felt angry and desolate all over again. What a Christmas Eve!

When she got to the porch, she turned to give her grandmother a limp wave. Grandma Rose waved back and began to hurry to her bus stop. Emily watched her go, not moving.

Then she had an idea, so sudden and daring that she threw her hands to her mouth.

She would follow her grandmother to work.

When she showed up, Grandma Rose would have no time to take her back home, and Mrs. Bigley would have to let her come in out of the bad weather.

And then, she could see Delilah.

In a flash, Emily ran down the porch steps and out the gate, then down the sidewalk after her grandmother. She came into sight of the bus stop just as Grandma Rose, in her bright red coat, began to climb onto a bus ahead of a short line of people. With a burst of speed, Emily raced to the stop and climbed in behind a large woman in a long coat.

Children ride free, she told herself. Everything's perfectly okay. But she could feel her heart pounding, hoping that Grandma Rose wouldn't see her yet!

Keeping the large woman between herself and her grandmother, Emily hurried down the aisle and sat toward the back, where she could watch Grandma Rose get off.

When the bus at last lurched away, Emily's heart lurched, too.

CHAPTER 3

What Does Delilah Want for Christmas?

"MY darling, I've been doing my very best to find you a wonderful Christmas present. Really, I have! There's just been nothing special enough."

I want—I want . . .

Mrs. Bigley leaned forward, holding her breath. "Tell me what you want, my love! I'll give you anything your heart desires, Delilah!"

The doll said nothing more.

Had she really said anything at all? Mrs. Bigley felt confused about this.

Delilah's blue glass eyes looked through Mrs. Bigley as though they didn't see her.

But surely they did, Mrs. Bigley thought desperately. "Look at me, Delilah!" she pleaded.

Delilah's china face remained stiff and cold in its frame of perfect dark ringlets.

"Oh, don't be angry with me!"

Mrs. Bigley snatched Delilah up and clutched the doll to her. Delilah, however, did not return the embrace. She never did, anymore. Hadn't she, though, long ago? Mrs. Bigley was sure of it.

It's my fault, it must be, she thought. What a terrible Christmas!

Mrs. Bigley had combed shops and catalogs for weeks without finding the right Christmas present for Delilah. If only she had a clue about what to get, where to look. . . . If only Delilah would just say, right out, what she wanted. Mrs. Bigley could surely find it, or find someone to make it!

So far, she had come across only second-rate versions of things Delilah already had.

Mrs. Bigley sat on the floor in front of the miniature Christmas tree in Delilah's sitting room, trying to think what to do next. Her breath stirred the tiny tinsel icicles, regular ones she'd had Rose cut down to the right size for a three-foot-high Christmas tree. The tree looked as beautiful as ever, from its handmade satin skirt to the exquisite porcelain angel on top. Miniature lights flashed among the tiny ornaments.

Under the tree lay a few little parcels Mrs. Bigley had managed to find earlier in the season. But they were nothings:

A miniature tin of miniature cookies
A tiny embroidered pillowcase
A little coloring book with tiny crayons
A jigsaw puzzle about four inches square
    with a hundred pieces.

Sweet toys, but unimportant. Delilah would

think nothing of them. Delilah had always, *always* had one big, exciting present.

Mrs. Bigley put the doll back in her silk-covered chair. Delilah's glassy eyes pierced her own.

Not good enough!

"Oh, I know! I know!" Mrs. Bigley wailed. "After so many lovely Christmases, I just don't know *why* I can't find anything this year."

But Mrs. Bigley could remember, she thought, a time when Delilah had graciously accepted her gifts, when she had been as sweet as—

You don't really love me at all, do you? It's all your fault. . . .

Mrs. Bigley pressed her hands to her ears. When had Delilah begun to speak to her like that? As if Mrs. Bigley hadn't blamed herself enough, all these years! Now her darling, the only one she had left, had taken up the old accusation.

Mrs. Bigley spoke sternly to herself, out loud. That sometimes stopped the other voice.

"I *will* find the best present yet! There's still time. Oh, if Rose would just hurry and come so I can get to the shops!"

Last year, Mrs. Bigley had given Delilah a tiny windup gramophone with a set of little records that really played. The year before that, she'd found a library of all of Grimm's fairy tales, hand-printed and colored, just the right size for Delilah's hands. The year before that, she had installed a train with a track, with one car to carry Delilah. Before that, she'd bought a real, working, miniature carousel.

A terrible thought occurred to Mrs. Bigley. Perhaps Delilah already had everything worth having . . .

Mrs. Bigley froze, then collected herself. Oh, if Delilah knew she'd thought that! She glanced guiltily at the doll, who stared past her at the Christmas tree.

There'd better be something under that tree in the morning! Something splendid!

Mrs. Bigley thought, There must be something she needs! She looked around. The long, high-ceilinged room where she sat now held Delilah's "house." Her living room, dining room, and kitchen, and her bedroom, sunroom, and bathroom had been laid out with clear spaces between them. Each of Delilah's rooms contained opulent furnishings exactly scaled to her eighteen-inch height.

That formed the "inside" of Delilah's house. A hallway in the big house connected it to another large room. Along the walls of the hallway, Rose and Mrs. Bigley had painted an avenue of trees for Delilah to travel down on her way to her own private "park" in another room. The park contained small silk trees and beds of little silk flowers, an ornate gazebo, a miniature swing set, the train and its station, the carousel, a croquet game set up on an artificial lawn, and a sandy area near a tiny pond with a real fountain that pumped real water. In the sand sat a Delilah-sized sand castle, crumbling since the time Mrs. Bigley had "helped" Delilah build it.

Delilah sat in the chair next to her bed, still

in her lace nightgown from the night before, with the same simpering smile she had worn for well over a hundred years. She looked down her dainty nose at all her possessions: furniture and china and silver, her crystal chandelier, tiny jewels and miniature paintings, embroidered cushions, silk dresses, lace underwear, toys, and the "food" Mrs. Bigley and Rose put before her on her polished walnut table three times a day.

Could it be true? Mrs. Bigley wondered. Could it be that Delilah didn't need anything? That her household was, after all these years, at last . . . complete?

She stole a glance at the doll, who glared back at her.

You lust haven't tried hard enough! I want—

"Yes?" Mrs. Bigley strained to hear. "What? What do you want? Please, tell me!"

I want . . . I want . . . I want the best present EVER!

Mrs. Bigley groaned and dropped her face into her hands. "*Where* is Rose!"

CHAPTER 4

Emily's Journey

*E*MILY, meanwhile, traveled across the wintry city, keeping her grandmother within sight. When she looked out the bus window, she could see street after street of houses, buildings, stores, and intersections all decorated for Christmas. The brighter they shone and glittered, the more she disliked them.

How could it ever be Christmas again, after what had happened last summer? How?

She turned her thoughts back to getting to see Delilah.

Whenever she thought about the doll, she felt she could, if she tried hard enough, become as small and precious as Delilah, surrounded by a world of treasures, where nothing would ever change. Where her heart could not be broken.

If only, if only . . .

The lady next to her broke into her thoughts. She nudged Emily, pointed out the window, and said, "Isn't it all just beautiful!" Emily nodded politely, fearing the woman would draw attention to her. She didn't want to talk.

But the woman continued. "What do you want for Christmas, sweetie?"

Emily had to answer. "I want . . . a doll," she replied. She felt she had come close enough to telling the truth.

"How nice! So few little girls seem to want dolls anymore. It's all computers and those music things. I like an old-fashioned Christmas! Can you guess what I'm going to pick up for my grandson today?"

"No, ma'am."

"A puppy! He's been wanting one for months."

Emily felt herself go pale. She turned her head toward the window and refused to speak after that. The woman made a few more attempts to draw her out, but gave up. She could not have chosen a more painful thing to say. A puppy!

Last summer, for her birthday, Emily had begged so long and stubbornly for a puppy that her parents had finally given in and agreed she could have one. When the day came to pick it up, they'd gone off laughing in the car, leaving Emily at a friend's.

On their way to get the puppy, the accident had happened.

She'd never seen them again.

She felt sick, remembering how hard she'd

begged for that dog, and hated herself all over again for it. The terrible thoughts began: *If only, if only . . .* She could hear herself, still:

"All I want for my birthday is a puppy!"

"Honey, we live in an apartment. A dog won't be happy here."

"A little one would be! I'll take care of it. You won't even know it's around."

"That's not the point, Emily. Someday we'll live in a house and then you can have a dog."

"I want a dog now! If I can't have one for my birthday, I don't want anything!"

Tears of shame came to her eyes now. If only she hadn't begged so hard, the accident would never have happened.

Suddenly she realized she'd been using that very same cross, pleading, insistent language. And very recently! The same tone of voice, the same argument . . .

She'd been behaving to her grandmother as she had to her parents!

What if this turned out as badly as the trip to get the puppy had?

What had she done?

Emily looked for her grandmother. I'll go to her and apologize, she thought.

But Grandma Rose was no longer in her seat.

Emily's heart jumped into her throat as she craned her neck to look for her. Her thoughts scrambled. If we get lost from each other—all my fault—oh, please!

At last she saw her grandmother, standing near the front of the braking bus.

"Excuse me, this is my stop." Emily pushed past knees and parcels. By the time she got into the aisle, a half dozen grown-ups had stepped between her and Grandma Rose, and Grandma Rose was out the door.

CHAPTER 5

Emily Tries to Catch Up

"GRANDMA! Grandma Rose!" Emily shouted. She shoved forward, trying to keep her in sight out the bus window. When she finally reached the sidewalk; Grandma Rose was half a block away.

Emily began to run, but had to stop at a red light. Her grandmother got farther and farther away, and the sounds of the city traffic and the wind overwhelmed Emily's shouts. The moment the light changed, she ran again,

24

but she couldn't catch up, though she could still see Grandma Rose's coat far ahead.

Emily's heart thumped like a huge drum through her chest and up into her throat. What if she lost sight of her grandmother? What had she done? What had she done?

Farther and farther ahead, Grandma Rose vanished around a corner. When Emily finally reached it, no one walked between them anymore. But her grandmother never once looked back. Emily called, but the wind snatched her voice away. And she was so out of breath, she had to stop running to shout, which put more distance between them.

Grandma Rose turned another corner. Emily struggled to follow.

That wind! And now, was it beginning to snow? Tiny needles of ice blew into her face.

The city seemed to have dropped away. Finally, she came alongside a long, black iron fence with posts like spears. Behind the fence, a thick wall of dark fir trees thrashed in the wind, roaring what sounded like warnings.

Then Grandma Rose disappeared.

On feet that felt like lumps of cold lead, Emily thudded on into the wind. Beside her, the trees moaned and shuddered, and the sky darkened with her rising fear. The ice needles blew faster into her face and stung her eyelids.

At last she came to a small gate left ajar. Grandma Rose must have turned in at that point, into a long, curving drive. Emily ran through the gate and down the drive. The red of her grandmother's coat flashed before disappearing around a curve ahead.

The grim forest crowded both sidesh of the drive. A dark stone tower with a pointed metal roof and windows soon appeared above it, disappearing and reappearing as Emily followed the twisting road. She ran past the trees, frightened of the way they stretched toward her, groaning and threatening. They held back the wind, but their roar covered the sound of her calls.

When Emily faced the gloomy, looming house at last, still so far away, she could see her grandmother unlocking an enormous door and disappearing into the house.

Emily fought the wind until she reached the door. She pushed the bell, but the button fell out into her mitten. She banged the heavy knocker, but she heard nothing from inside. No one came. She pounded and shouted. Nothing.

Finally, despairing, she turned away.

Grandma Rose was too far away to hear, Emily realized. She thought, I'll freeze to death out here.

And it would serve her right, too.

CHAPTER 6

Rose at Work

MRS. Bigley stood tapping her foot near the main door to the apartment at the top of the mansion, waiting. At last, a key turned in the lock, then another key in another lock, then the last. Out of breath, Rose staggered in, bringing a block of icy air with her.

"Ah, Rose, I'm glad you aren't *too* late. I must go out shopping. This is the last chance, and I still haven't found Delilah's special Christmas present."

Rose couldn't talk yet after her hard walk, and especially after climbing so many stairs. She began taking off her coat, but her fingers were too stiff to make much progress. She had to lean against the wall and take deep breaths, with Mrs. Bigley glaring at her the whole time.

When Rose could speak, she said, "I'm so sorry to be late, ma'am. But you mustn't go out! It's the coldest, windiest day I've ever seen. It's dangerous out there, really dangerous!"

Mrs. Bigley had pulled her own coat on in the meantime. "Nonsense! Besides, I'll be in the Bentley. You really should get a car, Rose."

Rose stared at her. Although Rose earned more money than most housekeepers, it wasn't enough for a car. Mrs. Bigley had never even given her a Christmas present.

She thought, You have no idea what it's like out there—you'll be back in five minutes. But she said only, "You know best, Mrs. Bigley." She flexed her fingers, willing them to warm up.

The old woman pulled on her gloves. "Please dress Delilah in her warmest dressing gown.

She's not looking very happy today. I hope she isn't coming down with something, just at Christmas."

Rose sighed. She finally got her coat unbuttoned and turned to speak. On the way to work, she had decided to ask Mrs. Bigley again, as a great favor, to let Emily come and see the doll. Just once, and only after Emily promised with all her heart never to tell anyone about Delilah. If the old woman wouldn't agree . . . well, maybe it was time Rose found another job.

Her heart fluttered at the thought, though. Rose knew she could not earn nearly as much money as a housekeeper anywhere else. And the sad, old woman—she was so crazy. She really needed Rose to look after her.

Before Rose could say anything, Mrs. Bigley had her gloves and scarf on and her purse in her hand. The old woman announced, "Yes, poor Delilah! You'd better set her in the sunroom with a shawl. Be sure to leave her a glass of water, and a handkerchief, and something to read on the table next to the chaise longue. I'll see you later."

Rose sighed. Of course she wouldn't quit, so she wouldn't ask. But she couldn't let Mrs. Bigley go out there in that weather.

She spoke up again. "I think Delilah will be very frightened to think of you out in this terrible storm."

This caught Mrs. Bigley's attention. She paused by the door and looked at Rose, biting her lip. Then she called out to the doll, "I'm just running an errand, my dear. Santa needs my help today, just for a little while." She pulled the door open and hurried out.

Rose shook her head and put away her own things, then threaded her way through the miniature furniture to Delilah. The doll stared up at her. "What foolishness," Rose said. Then she realized she'd spoken to a doll. I'd better watch out or I'll get crazy, too! she thought.

Rose bent to pick up Delilah and begin her day's work.

How her knees hurt! She wondered how

Mrs. Bigley, so much older, could get up and down so easily.

As she pulled Delilah's dressing gown over the doll's cold china arms, she wondered what had gone so very, very wrong for Mrs. Bigley. What could it have been?

CHAPTER 7

Locked Out!

EMILY, meanwhile, feeling more frozen and desperate by the moment, had gone around a corner of the house to get out of the worst of the wind, when she suddenly heard the sound of an engine. Shouting and waving, she ran toward the big car as it drove away, but it soon left her far behind.

She'd seen a head barely tall enough to see over the steering wheel. It must have been Mrs. Bigley, she realized. How did she get out of the house? Maybe she left a door unlocked.

Emily ran to the back of the house. The garage door, finished rolling down. It had no handle. A terrace ran across nearly the entire back of the house. She ran up the stone steps and along the wall of well-boarded-up windows and glass doors that separated the terrace from the house, pounding and yelling, but nothing happened. She went down the stairs on the other side and found another, door, but it, too, absorbed her knocking without any result. She couldn't reach even the bottom of the rest of the windows.

She hurried back to the front door and pounded again, shouting for Grandma Rose.

No one came.

Despairing, Emily turned away again. She knew she wouldn't remember the way back to the bus stop—she'd kept her eyes on her grandmother, not on her surroundings. She might get on the wrong bus, if she found one at all. She would end up even more lost.

She must stay here and try to get inside to Grandma Rose.

Emily shook with the cruel cold as she headed around to the side of the house she hadn't yet searched. She couldn't find another entrance on that side, which was protected by thick, overgrown holly bushes. It reminded her of Sleeping Beauty's castle.

Then she noticed, behind the bushes, a row of basement windows, each in a stone-lined well full of dead leaves. She struggled through the holly, protecting her face, until she got to the nearest one. She climbed into the well and tried to pull up the window, but it didn't budge.

Emily fought her tears as she sank back into a corner of the window well. Her last hope had gone nowhere.

At least the well protected her from the wind and icy snow, and the leaves actually gave her a little warmth. She tucked her frozen face down and tried to think. No crying, just thinking, she warned herself.

She had to get inside.

So, she had to break the window.

But that would be wrong.

But if she didn't, she'd freeze, maybe to death.

She could break the window and tell Mrs. Bigley she'd pay for it.

With what? She only had about twelve dollars in the whole world. How much does a window cost, Emily wondered.

The wind suddenly blew even louder. Emily made up her mind. She stood up to look for anything heavy enough to throw against the window. The cold tore into her, and she squatted down again.

This time she spoke out loud. "I *have* to do it! It's too, too, too cold!" She gathered her courage and stood again, clambered out of the well, and fought her way back out through the holly. She searched the ground until she found a large, jagged rock. She struggled with it back into the window well.

Now!

She leaned down and pounded the glass. It was much harder to do than she had thought, but the glass broke at last. She beat at it and then smashed the places around the frame where jagged bits poked out.

Now she could see down into the darkness.

Such *dark* darkness.

Jump! she told herself.

But what if she fell on broken glass?

She put her head close to the opening and shouted, "Grandma Rose! Grandma Rose!" The sound got swallowed in the darkness.

Grimly she told herself, I *must* get inside.

The dark hole gaped at her, and she shuddered. She hated darkness. She hadn't slept without a light on in her room since her parents—since *then*. She couldn't remember what they looked like, in the darkness.

Emily looked through the shrubbery at the thrashing, groaning trees, up at the sky that had lowered and darkened even more since she'd gotten off the bus. She stamped her feet and rubbed her frozen hands together and tried again to think of some other way.

Then she sat, put her legs through the opening, turned onto her stomach, and pushed herself through the window, letting herself drop.

CHAPTER 8

The Perfect Present

MRS. Bigley drove through the shopping district she had already searched for so many weeks, feeling defeated. Once again she had not found the right present. She knew the last-minute shoppers would have picked over what was left. In her concentration, she barely noticed the cold or that she had forgotten lunch.

She drove along, looking for a shop she might not have noticed before, and came to an unfamiliar corner. She would drive down this one last street and if she hadn't found anything by the end of the block, she'd give up. She thought, what shall I tell Delilah? She'll be so disappointed tomorrow, so . . . angry.

Mrs. Bigley spied a brightly lit window and pulled alongside it. To her disappointment, the sign said

VICKI'S PETS

Nothing for Delilah there!

Before she drove on, another sign in the pet shop window caught her eye:

THE WORLD'S TINIEST DOG

Mrs. Bigley braked hard. She stared out at the shop window, but she couldn't see anything clearly. Noticing a parking space, she maneuvered her enormous car into it and clambered out. The cold took her breath away as she hurried across the street to the shop.

Below the sign in the window, a large china teacup sat by itself on a bed of draped green velvet. Quite a nice teacup, Mrs. Bigley noticed with approval, real bone china, banded in gold, with a dainty pattern of roses. She moved closer to the window to get a look inside the cup.

There, curled up, a tiny, fluffy, white dog slept with its shiny, black nose resting on teeny front paws. As Mrs. Bigley watched, the little animal began to dream. It wrinkled its little snout and—she imagined, since she couldn't hear through the glass—gave a series of little barks. At the same time, its front and back paws began to twitch.

Mrs. Bigley stared, entranced. Suddenly, the dog shook himself awake, sat up in his teacup, and looked her right in the face.

Both of them froze. And perhaps because he stayed so still, so like a doll himself, Mrs. Bigley said right out loud, "Why, you're *exactly* the right size for Delilah! And Delilah needs a pet!"

As soon as she had said this—and the thought had never occurred to her before—it felt like the truth. Delilah had several small stuffed animals, including a dog. She had a miniature Noah's ark and some little books about animals, but a real dog—

Just the thing!

Mrs. Bigley hurried up the steps and pulled the door open against the wind.

The warm shop felt and looked like a tropical island in the middle of the wintry city. Gurgling aquariums, flutterings and whistlings in a floor-to-ceiling birdcage, and strange cries greeted her. A gaudy parrot sidestepped on its perch and called, "Hi, babe!" and whistled. Mrs. Bigley jumped, then scowled at him. A box of twitchy rabbits caught her eye, as did a large glass case full of kittens romping with one another.

Mrs. Bigley stood bewildered at the sight of so much liveliness. She had forgotten why she had come in.

A slender young woman with curls gathered into a messy clump on her head walked out of the back, smiling. "May I help you?"

Mrs. Bigley couldn't speak. The sight of the young woman confused her even more. The thought leaped into her mind: I know someone who looks like that!

The young woman looked more closely at her. "Did you just come in to get warm? It's certainly terrible weather! Can I get you something hot to drink?"

Wake up, silly fool, Mrs. Bigley told herself. But who is it? Who does she remind me of?

"Please," she croaked, her voice funny after the cold. She looked around helplessly for a moment. Then from behind the velvet-draped glass of the window display, she heard a tiny bark—"Quiff!"—and remembered.

She took a deep breath. "I want to buy the little dog in your display."

The young woman's warm smile faded. "Oh. You mean Teacup."

"Teacup?"

"That's what I've been calling him."

Neither woman spoke. The young woman looked unhappy.

Finally Mrs. Bigley said coldly, "May I see him? He *is* for sale, isn't he?"

"Oh. Yes, of course." The young woman sighed and edged past Mrs. Bigley. She leaned over the display case. "Teacup! Here, boy! Come on!" Then she turned toward Mrs. Bigley.

The old woman caught her breath. Up close in the young woman's hands, the little dog looked even more adorable than he had in the window. He sat in her cupped palms, looking at Mrs. Bigley with his head cocked, one tiny ear flopping over one sparkling dot of an eye.

"Goodness," Mrs. Bigley said. "He *is* small."

"He's a real dog, though. He's the runt of the litter of really tiny parents of a super-miniature breed. But he's strong and healthy. He may grow a bit, but not much more. Would you like to hold him?"

Mrs. Bigley slowly held out her gloved hands. Teacup leaned forward and sniffed them. Then he sat down and scratched himself behind the neck in a quick blur.

"Call him," the young woman suggested.

"Come here, Teacup," Mrs. Bigley said softly.

Teacup bounded over to her and landed softly in her palms. Mrs. Bigley swayed at the odd feeling of something so alive in her hands. Teacup looked into her face and barked twice: "Quiff! Quiff!"

"What a . . . sweet sound!" Mrs. Bigley brought him carefully up to her cheek. She felt the warm breeze of his breath, the tickle of his minute whiskers, and then a definite, though miniature, doggy kiss. "Well!" she said, and looked wonderingly at the young woman.

"He needs a very special home. He's quite an unusual dog. The breeders decided they couldn't keep him with the larger dogs, so they asked me to find him a good place. And of course, he's very expensive."

Mrs. Bigley suddenly understood that the young woman didn't want to sell the dog.

She tightened her hold on the pup just a

bit, frightened that she might not get to take him home to Delilah after all.

"I assure you," she said in a tight voice, "I have the *perfect* home for, uh . . . Teacup. He'll have everything he needs and more. I feel as though I've been looking for him for years. He is exactly the right size for . . . for our needs. How much do you want for him?"

The price nearly made Mrs. Bigley step back.

The young woman moved toward Mrs. Bigley, smiling now, stretching out her hands to take Teacup back.

But Mrs. Bigley clutched him closer. "That is rather high, but I *must* have him." Already she was imagining Teacup lying on Delilah's lap, sitting obediently at her side, walking on a tiny leash as Mrs. Bigley pulled the doll in her little wagon. Yes, Delilah could wear her sailor dress, with her high-buttoned shoes.

The young woman saw her determination and sighed. "All right."

Buying Teacup, Mrs. Bigley discovered,

took more than just writing a check. She bought kibble and little dishes. The young woman gave her Teacup's veterinary record and papers. She found a warm blanket to line the box in which he would travel to Mrs. Bigley's home.

Mrs. Bigley's hands trembled with excitement as she took possession of her purchases. Teacup's box had a tight lid and little holes so that he could get air, but he was well protected from the cold.

On the way home at last, with the box on the seat next to her, Mrs. Bigley found herself singing a Christmas carol. She caught a glimpse of her happy, relieved, animated face in the rearview mirror and realized, Oh! *I* used to look just like that girl!

Then she drove the rest of the way home in silence.

CHAPTER *9*

Lost in the Dark

EMILY landed in a crouch on a concrete floor. She had fallen so far that she thought at first she must have gotten hurt, but gradually she began to move and realized she had't broken or sprained anything. Better yet, although her shoes crunched on broken glass, she had no cuts.

She stayed hunkered down on the floor, very still and listening hard. She could hear nothing but her own throbbing heart and breath. A bit of gray light leaked through the window, along with a lot of cold air gushing down on her. As her eyes adjusted to the dark, she noted the bareness of the room, seeing only a mousetrap in the nearest corner. She could just make out a tiny skeleton in it.

What if she couldn't get out of here? What if she died down here and they found *her* skeleton years from now?

She began to whimper. She knew she couldn't reach the window ledge behind her, and the room held nothing she could climb on to get out the way she'd come in.

"I'm trapped, I'm trapped," she moaned. Then she thought, No! Stop it! Stop it! Find Grandma Rose and get warm and be safe! Stop crying and get moving!

She spoke out loud to herself, "See? Have some sense. Be glad you're indoors." Her voice, though hollow and echoing in the empty gloom, gave her courage. She listened harder, holding her breath. She pictured—her grandmother, somewhere in this house, hurrying through her work. Imagining Emily safe in day care. Emily spoke out loud once more. "I will find you, Grandma Rose!"

She tried to figure out what to do. She know her grandmother worked at the top of the house. Find stairs!

Emily could just make out the door, which stood barely ajar. She opened the door into a deeper darkness, forcing herself to go into what seemed to be a corridor.

Again she called for her grandmother. Her voice echoed, a tiny, frightened thing that seemed to cling to the air right around her. No one could hear that, Emily knew.

Straining her ears, she thought she heard a scuttling sound far down the corridor to her right. Mouse? Rat? Emily closed her eyes and prayed she wouldn't have to deal with anything as nasty as a rat. She listened harder. Nothing. Some tears squeezed through her tight eyelids. She had to let go of this doorknob and look for Grandma Rose.

The room behind her now seemed safe and

known. She didn't want to leave the puny scrap of light that leaked through its window, and she didn't want to set off all alone into this huge, unknown house. Or, worse, to set off with rats and mice scurrying around. Or other things that she didn't want to think about at all. With all her heart, she didn't want to go forward. With all her mind, she knew she couldn't go back.

Only once before had she felt so terribly, utterly alone. A sob lurched from her chest, but she managed to tell herself, No! Don't think about them now. Find Grandma Rose!

If she left this door wide open, she'd get all the light she could. If only she had a string or something to tie to it, so she could find her way back!

She thought then of her mittens, knit by her grandmother. Lots of string there! Taking one off, she tried to find a loose end, but Grandma Rose had finished her work well. Emily leaned against the door frame and bit into the top edge of the mitten until she felt the yarn tear in that place. She caught a frayed end and pulled it hard. It gathered up as she pulled, then suddenly the yarn broke. When it did, the bottom few rows of knitting fell away. She made her stiff fingers work at the raw edge, and finally a long strand came loose. It would now unravel quickly, she knew. Emily tied the end to the doorknob and took a deep breath. She put her cold bare hand into her pocket, holding the raveling mitten with her other hand, and turned to the left.

In ten steps she had entered nearly complete darkness. In fifteen, she found another door and opened it. Grateful, she stood looking toward its high window, which seemed bright after the darkness. That room, too, stood entirely empty. She left the door open and went on.

When she came to a wall, she had to turn to her right. She thought she heard, again, somewhere ahead, a tiny scurrying. She moved on, one hand trailing the wall, telling herself to the rhythm of her steps and heartbeat, "I'm coming, Grandma Rose! I'm coming, Grandma Rose!"

She wondered again if she should try to shout, but decided not to, saving her voice until she got closer. She took several turns and opened a few more doors, none of which, however, had windows. Every step took her into deeper darkness.

"Ouch!"

She had bumped right into a wall, hitting her head. She felt her way along it. Then it came to a stop. No, not a stop. It had a top edge that she could tell ran up to the left and down to the right.

A staircase! Yes! The way upstairs!

Emily hurried around to the bottom of the stairs and peered upward, but the darkness gave her no help. She still had quite a bit of yarn left in her mitten.

She started to climb.

CHAPTER 10

Teacup's New Home

WHEN she returned from her shopping expedition, Mrs. Bigley looked more excited than Rose had ever seen her. She surprised Rose even more by smiling—no, grinning!—at her. She put down her purse, a sack, and the large parcel she carried. "Help me out of my things, Rose, I'm frozen. Oh, just *wait* until you see what I've found for Delilah!"

Rose wiped her hands on her apron as she walked over the thick carpet toward Mrs.

Bigley. How could the old woman have borne to go out in weather like that? And she could not imagine what had made Mrs. Bigley so happy.

What could she possibly have found for the doll? Let it be easy to dust, she prayed.

Mrs. Bigley almost danced with excitement. "Try to guess, Rose, just try!"

Rose finally got Mrs. Bigley disentangled from her scarf. "I don't know, ma'am." She shook her head. "Really, I can't guess."

Then she noticed the pet shop's name on the parcel and paused. What has she done? Rose wondered. Oh, not an animal, please not!

Timidly, she asked, "Did you get . . . a little bird?"

Mrs. Bigley gave her a twinkling smile and slowly, teasingly began pulling open the box. "Wrong! Oh, you'll never guess!" She beckoned Rose nearer, and when she had the carton opened, tilted it toward her.

Rose, still confused by Mrs. Bigley's gaiety, at first could not take in what she saw. In the bottom of the box, something small, white, and fluffy looked up at her. Some kind of curly coated rat? She jumped back. "Wha—"

"It's a *dog*, of course! His name is Teacup. He's a real, nearly full-grown dog. And just exactly the right size for Delilah." Rose had never heard Mrs. Bigley sound so happy and young.

Who had ever heard of a dog so small? Mrs. Bigley must be imagining things. Someone at that pet shop had taken advantage of a crazy old woman and sold her some kind of rat! Rose recovered herself and peered again into the carton.

A tiny dog stared up at her. *A dog!*

Rose gaped at Mrs. Bigley. "How? . . . What? . . ."

During all this, Teacup sat looking from one face to the other. Then he stood up, shook himself, stretched toward Rose in a way that looked like a bow, and gave two sharp little barks: "Quiff! Quiff!" Mrs. Bigley reached inside and held out her hand, which Teacup sniffed before dancing onto it.

Mrs. Bigley presented him to Rose.

Rose, scarcely daring to breathe, put out a finger to him. The little dog sniffed it, and then gave it a tiny lick.

"He's . . . real." Rose still couldn't get over it. Her heart went out to the tiny creature. "Oh, he's precious!"

Mrs. Bigley's eyes shone. "I can hardly wait to give him to Delilah! In fact—I can't wait. I know she would rather have Teacup now than wait another whole day for Christmas. Besides, I can't bear to keep him in this box."

Mrs. Bigley started for Delilah's sunroom, holding Teacup in front of her as if he were being offered to a god—or goddess, in this case.

Rose followed her, fascinated.

Delilah lay on her wicker chaise longue, partly covered with a dainty afghan. Her half-closed eyes made her look as fretful as if she really did have a headache. Next to her, a little glass-topped wicker table held a small crystal goblet of water and her tiny silver pillbox. One hand "gripped" a lace handkerchief, while the other rested on an open, miniature edition of *Little Women*.

"Look what Santa's brought you, my darling," Mrs. Bigley crooned. "I ran into him in town. He made a special trip, just for you, since you haven't been feeling well." She knelt on the floor and hid her hands, with Teacup, in her skirt. Then she brought the little dog out and held him in front of Delilah's face. "Merry, merry Christmas! Your very own, real, true, little dog!"

She placed Teacup on the afghan and leaned back. Rose knelt, too, and to her astonishment, Mrs. Bigley's hand found and clasped one of her own. Rose squeezed back. For once, she came close to sharing Mrs. Bigley's fantasy about Delilah.

Teacup gave a little shake, scratched behind his neck, looked around, and then leaned forward to sniff Delilah's porcelain face. He sniffed for a long time, as though puzzled. Then, so quickly neither woman could tell how it had happened, he jumped off Delilah, off the chaise longue, and scampered away.

"Oh!" cried Mrs. Bigley. "Oh my!" She clung to Rose's hand. "He's running *away*! From *Delilah*!"

Rose couldn't take her eyes off Teacup racing through the doll's house.

"Rose, he mustn't! Oh, help me!" Mrs. Bigley struggled to stand up.

Rose helped her. "Calm down, ma'am." They began to try to follow Teacup through the maze of doll furniture.

Teacup ran like a sprite, poking his tiny nose into Delilah's wardrobe, jumping on and off her bed, then out of her bedroom to Delilah's kitchen, where he at first barked at and then ignored a small china kitten in its basket by the stove.

Rose and Mrs. Bigley hurried as fast as they could after him, but couldn't keep up. Down the hall again he raced, and into the doll-sized bathroom, jumping into and out of Delilah's bathtub, sniffing her tiny jar of bath crystals and the little sponge. Then he ran back to the sunroom where Delilah still sat, vacantly looking from under her arched, painted eyebrows.

This time, after scratching behind his ear in a furious blur, Teacup ran right up to Delilah, caught a corner of the afghan in his mouth, and yanked it off her.

Mrs. Bigley, two doll rooms away, saw this and stumbled forward, horrified.

Rose giggled. She didn't mean to, and she covered her mouth with her hands so that Mrs. Bigley wouldn't see, but Teacup fighting with the afghan made a funny sight.

Teacup backed away from the chaise longue with the afghan in his mouth, growling and shaking it. That was bad enough! But, as both Mrs. Bigley and Rose realized at the same moment, Delilah had been well tucked up in the afghan, and Teacup was pulling her sideways. She now tilted toward the glass-topped table edge. Before either woman could reach her, Teacup gave a final yank and Delilah lost her balance entirely. Her head struck the edge of the table, and she and the table tipped over onto the floor.

Mrs. Bigley cried out. The tiny goblet spilled water onto Delilah's book. The table rolled until the edge of its round glass top was stopped by Delilah's head. The pillbox rolled out of sight.

Teacup ran away.

CHAPTER 11

A Princess's Bedroom

EMILY had reached the end of her rope. The end of her yarn, that is. She stood looking into a long, very dark corridor, holding the last bit of yarn from her second mitten. It seemed to her that she had been searching the enormous, frigid house forever. She had no idea where in the house she had ended up, but she had climbed higher and higher, knowing her grandmother worked at the very top.

And all that time, she had let her mittens

unravel behind her, a long thread of hope that she could use to retrace her steps and find her way back to the broken window.

Now she realized how *much* hope that had given her. Because now she had to decide whether to let go of it or not.

And—so far—she could not.

She felt tired, cold to the core, hungry, and very thirsty. She had opened taps in all the bathrooms she had come to, but none of them worked. Still, she had used a toilet, so at least she didn't have *that* discomfort.

At last she had started calling and shouting for her grandmother—until her voice had worn out in the freezing, dusty, dry air of the mansion. Now she couldn't call out even if Grandma Rose suddenly appeared!

Should she go forward into yet another long, dark corridor? Or try to go back, climb out the window, and go for help? *Any* help. She'd had so many disappointments! So many corridors had seemed to her that they *must* lead to Grandma Rose. . . .

How much more disappointment could she take before she just lay down on the floor and went to sleep and—then what?

But to go back! Such a long way back!

And what if the yarn had broken some-where along the way? What if she only reached another end, in another dark place? Emily shuddered.

At least I'm up a lot higher now, she told herself. Maybe at the top of the house. She stood a minute longer, then dropped the end of the yarn and began to walk. She *must* be closer now!

The corridor turned and twisted, some-times taking her through a stretch of nearly complete darkness, so that she had to touch the walls as she walked along. She felt she had never used her eyes so hard. When she came to a door, she opened it, with the usual results.

Then at last one dim corridor went on without doors farther than any she had trav-eled, on and on and on, getting darker and darker. Or maybe it only seemed longer than all the others, since she went more and more slowly into the deepening murk, missing her little strand of yarn. She kept her hand against the wall, but that didn't stop her from bumping into another wall that she hadn't been able to see. She hit her forehead quite hard.

Tears came to her eyes. At least so far, she had managed not to hurt herself! She put both arms out toward the wall she had collided with and felt along it, letting tears—blessedly warm—roll down her cheeks.

The wall ended abruptly. She felt around the corner, and her hands found a doorknob.

This doorknob felt different from the rest. Larger and heavier, and not round but with corners, like a cut-glass pitcher her grandmother treasured. She peered, but could not see it. She imagined it as a giant polished jewel.

Would it turn?

Yes.

She opened the door.

Thin winter light pierced her eyes. Even so little light made her blink after so much darkness.

Something else was different. This room had furniture in it—not a jumble of old junk heaped up, but real furniture! She stood and let her eyes adjust. She had arrived *somewhere*.

The light came from the cracks between the many shutters that encircled the room.

She must be in the tower!

She could see, now, in the center of the room, a canopied bed on a marble platform. As she drew nearer to it, the elaborate carvings on its pillars—unicorns, elves, trees, castles— seemed to come to life. Emily walked around it, tracing the carvings with her finger.

Not dusty, she noticed. She remembered that her grandmother had said Mrs. Bigley sometimes took cleaning supplies with her when she went into the locked-off part of the house.

She went across the room and tugged at one of the shutters, pulling it open to reveal only dense snow raging through the air. She looked at it until she felt dizzy, then turned back into the room.

A chandelier more beautiful than any she had ever imagined hung from a ceiling painted like the sky. The eight-sided room had windows on six sides, doors on two. Emily had come in through a double door. She crossed to the single door and opened it onto a bathroom as large as her grandmother's living room, with a swan-shaped bathtub in the middle.

She ran to the sink and turned a tap. To her joy, water—beautiful water!—gushed out. She cupped her hand under it, not wanting to damage the delicate crystal goblet on the counter, and drank and drank and drank.

She drank a little more, and when she lifted her head again, she saw her face in the mirror. She looked pale and dirty, with streaks of dust across her face. She pushed up her sleeves and splashed herself clean, but couldn't bring herself to use the rich, white hanging next to her. Instead, she wiped her face with her sleeve and went back into the bedroom.

She could see well now and, standing in the center of the room, she turned slowly in a circle and stared. The shutters had elaborate paintings of fairy-tale scenes. Dwarfs waved good-bye to Snow White, who was leaning out a window. Three pigs smiled in the doorway of a neat brick cottage. A pretty young woman helped a swan put on a shirt. Two children approached a house made of pastries and candies. A pumpkin-shaped coach rolled toward a castle. A boy climbed a beanstalk that seemed to disappear through a hole in the sky-painted ceiling. . . .

Between the windows, fantastic carved trees sent branches up into the ceiling. The rest of the room gleamed with silver and gold. The bed itself, covered in soft pillows, glowed from a gold silk comforter.

Emily climbed up to the bed, then reached out and stroked the comforter. She felt its thick softness.

Then she pulled it down, pushed some of the many pillows out of the way, and climbed onto the bed. She struggled with her boots and got them off, but her hands, still cold, couldn't manage to undo her shoes, so she left them on. *I'll just get warm. Warm.*

She lay down, pulled up the comforter, and fell asleep.

CHAPTER 12

Delilah's Disaster

MRS. Bigley reached Delilah first and began to pick her up. Just then, she heard a crash from Delilah's dining room.

She stood up at once. "Rose! Help!" She pointed at the table, where Teacup had pulled the tablecloth, along with all the china and crystal and silver decorations, onto the floor.

But Rose stood rooted, her apron to her mouth, shaking with helpless laughter.

Teacup had run away after the crash and

tried to hide in the bathtub under a towel his leap had pulled down.

Mrs. Bigley turned to Rose, her eyes wide and her mouth open as if she were about to cry. Rose stifled her laughter, hoping Mrs. Bigley would think her own tears had erupted out of concern.

The old woman didn't seem to notice she'd left Delilah facedown on the carpet. To Rose's surprise, she took a deep breath, pulled herself upright, and began walking carefully toward Teacup. Away from Delilah!

Teacup peeked up at Mrs. Bigley from under his towel. His tail began to wag furiously as she leaned over and reached for him. Just in time, he shook off the towel, scampered to the other end of the tub, and jumped out.

"Why, you little . . . scamp!" cried Mrs. Bigley. "I do believe you think this is a game!"

And so he did. Try as they might, their size and age made Mrs. Bigley and Rose too clumsy and slow to catch him, especially since he kept overturning more and more of Delilah's furniture into their pathways, which also gave him dozens of hiding places and avenues for escape. After fifteen minutes, both women puffed with exhaustion, but Teacup's little "Quiff! Quiff!" sounded as lively as ever. The doll's house lay in a terrible mess.

Finally, Mrs. Bigley couldn't chase him any more. She leaned against the wall and looked around at the mess.

Rose caught up to her at last. Both women struggled to catch their breath.

Finally, Rose said, "Ma'am. Ma'am, I'm . . . I'm sorry." She held Delilah with the doll's face pressed against her dress front. She swallowed. "I don't know how to tell you—"

Mrs. Bigley didn't understand at first. Then her eyes widened. She reached for the doll, shaking her head. "Oh! Oh no. She's not—He didn't—"

She took Delilah from Rose and turned her around. The doll's nose had a piece missing, and a long crack split the smirking smile, ran up one cheek, and branched into two cracks alongside her right eye. The mechanism that made the eyes open and close could be plainly seen in the darkness inside Delilah's hollow head.

Mrs. Bigley stood holding her for a long, long time, staring at the ruined face.

At last, Rose touched her shoulder. "Mrs. Bigley? Ma'am?"

Mrs. Bigley did not seem to have heard.

Rose tried again. "Surely . . . surely she can be glued. Don't you think?"

Mrs. Bigley turned toward the sound of her voice, her eyes filling.

Rose reached for Delilah. "Maybe I can fix it. Her. With some glue . . . Or . . . or . . . we could work on it together!"

"No." Mrs. Bigley's voice sounded cold and flat and strange.

"But—"

"No." Mrs. Bigley began to back away. "*No!*"

Rose stopped. I must be very careful, she thought. "No, of course not. But let's go into the kitchen and sit down and think what to do. Come with me." With great care, she stepped toward Mrs. Bigley and took her arm.

The older woman began to wail.

"NO! NO! NO! NO! NO!" She shoved the doll at Rose and stumbled away. "What have I done? I've done it again! Oh! Not again!" she wailed.

Rose couldn't keep up with her as Mrs. Bigley fled through the mess, somehow not tripping. When the old woman reached the door that led into the tower and pulled a key from her pocket, Rose was too far behind to reach her. Mrs. Bigley grappled with the lock, pulled the heavy door open, and disappeared into the gloom beyond.

Rose got to the door just as it slammed shut and locked.

CHAPTER *13*

Rose Worries and Works

ROSE pulled Delilah close to her chest and squeezed her. She remembered Mrs. Bigley telling her once that she'd had the doll her whole life! It had belonged to her grandmother.

Poor thing, she thought. The poor old women! She tried the knob again, but it didn't turn. She pressed her ear to it but could hear nothing. She knocked, softly at first, then hard. "Mrs. Bigley! Mrs. Bigley!" she called.

No answer.

Rose turned with a sigh and surveyed Delilah's house. What a mess! She walked through the rooms, down the corridor, and into the park. The sand castle had vanished into a heap Evidently, the little dog liked to dig. Drops of water led away from the pond. She followed them as far as she could, calling for the pup, but couldn't find him.

Where could he be? In such a mess, he could get hurt. Rose's head began to ache with this new worry.

She turned the doll over in her arms and examined her. Delilah now looked ridiculous, with her eyes peering in different directions. Rose gently pressed the face until the cracks could close, but a piece of forehead then broke and fell into the hollow skull. She would never be the same.

Rose set Delilah on a little sofa, then thought better of it and put her up on Mrs. Bigley's dresser, where the dog would not be able to reach her. She went through Delilah's rooms, setting furniture upright and picking up objects that had fallen or that Teacup had carried from one place to another. She put broken pieces in her apron until she'd filled it, then set them on the kitchen table and went back to work.

As she cleaned, Rose kept an eye out for Teacup, but never saw him. "I suppose you've found someplace snug to take a nap, eh?" she called softly. Then she thought of a way to lure him out. She went to Mrs. Bigley's kitchen and fixed him some food and water and placed them on the floor in a corner away from the door. "When you get hungry enough, you'll come looking," she said. "And I'll shut you in here."

But he didn't appear.

CHAPTER *14*

Mrs. Bigley's Discovery

MRS. Bigley pulled the door behind her until she heard its lock click. She leaned against it, trembling from head to foot.

She could feel and hear Rose pounding and calling from the other side of the door. She stumbled along the corridor, holding the wall for support. The thickness of the door made Rose sound distant, but Mrs. Bigley could not get far enough from what she had just seen.

She felt as though a bandage over her deepest wound had been suddenly and cruelly ripped off.

"Delilah! Delilah!" she sobbed.

She pushed forward in the darkness of the corridor. The pain gathered inside her and grew.

She did have a place where pain could not reach her—if she just could get there. She suddenly felt so very old. She hobbled on more slowly.

She turned the last corner to her special, secret place. Now she felt really ill, but not too much to notice that the double door stood ajar. She paused, baffled and frightened, wondering what it could mean.

Then she realized who must have opened the doors she always shut so carefully. Her heart swelled with joy and hope. "Oh!" she cried. "Oh, at last!"

She stepped across the corridor and pulled the doors wide open and stepped inside. Now, although she still felt light-headed and sick, sadness and pain could not find her. She turned slowly, looking around the room.

"Delilah!" she said, her voice a funny, croaking whisper. "Oh, where are you? I know you must be here!" She continued to scan the room. "I—I had the worst dream—or something. . . . I dreamed you were . . . smashed up. D-dead. But you aren't! You found your way home! Where are you?"

Something in the bed moved.

Mrs. Bigley grasped a bedpost. A dark braid had snaked out onto the comforter. A child's head—

She reached out and tried to call, but the shock had overwhelmed her voice. Dizziness drove her to the floor. She looked up into the summer-sky ceiling until a great black cloud blotted everything out of her sight.

CHAPTER 15

Rose's Discovery

AFTER working awhile longer, Rose again knocked on the door Mrs. Bigley had gone through. She called and called to her. Getting no response, she turned back to the mess the little dog had made. None of her work seemed to have made much difference. She wandered through the clear paths, feeling more tired and worried. She put Mrs. Bigley's outdoor things into the closet by the door to the stairs and leaned against the thick press of clothes inside to shut it.

In the kitchen, she made a pot of tea. Then she looked at the wall clock. Two thirty! Where had the day gone? No wonder she felt so hungry! And Mrs. Bigley must be hungry, too.

She had hoped to leave by now. She'd better call the day care and let them know she wouldn't be coming as early as she had thought.

Rose hurried to the old black phone that squatted on the counter and dialed the number. The line sounded funny, full of crackles. Must be the storm, she thought. When Mrs. Debbs, the director, answered, Rose could hardly hear her. She spoke as slowly and loudly as she could.

"Mrs. Debbs, this is Rose Miller. I told you I thought I could pick Emily up early today, but I'm afraid my employer is . . . " Rose struggled to think what to say about this situation. ". . . is sick, and I'm going to be later than that. Would you tell Emily, please?"

Through the buzzes and whistles on the line, Rose could barely make out what Mrs. Debbs said. She pushed the phone more snugly to her ear. "Mrs. Debbs, I can't hear you!"

". . . haven't seen her . . . thought you . . . day off."

Rose's heart stood still. "*What?*" she shouted. She spoke as loudly and carefully as she could. "What are you saying? This is Rose Miller, Emily's grandmother. I brought Emily this morning!"

Through the noise on the line, she heard: ". . . only three children . . . terrible weather . . . haven't seen Emily . . . sure? . . . worried now . . . "

Rose felt as though the air and light had been sucked out of the room. She could hardly speak for anxiety, but took a deep breath and shouted, "YES or NO, is Emily with you?"

Buzz—"NO"—*crack-whistle*—"NO—"

The line went dead.

Rose started shaking. She stared at the phone in disbelief and let the receiver drop.

What had happened?

Desperate, she questioned her memory. Had she not taken Emily to day care?

Yes, of course she had! They'd struggled through that terrible wind.

She tried to recall seeing Emily going inside. No, that hadn't happened. She'd been in such a rush, she had just waved to her.

She saw Emily in her mind's eye, waving from the front porch.

But she could not recollect seeing Emily go inside the house. She had turned away too soon.

Then she knew: Emily had never gone inside!

Where was she?

CHAPTER *16*

Teacup Finds His Way

EARLIER, Teacup had found the closet where Mrs. Bigley kept her clothes. In the darkness, surrounded by boxes and shoes, he couldn't hear the women fussing anymore. What's more, he had found an old furry slipper. What a great enemy! Growling and rolling, flipping it over, fighting his way inside it and then outside again—he'd never had so much fun! He tussled with it for a good, long time, and then crawled into it to rest.

He sighed deeply and settled farther down into the slipper, his nose resting on its heel. Now that he had found a quiet place, though, he began to feel lonely. As interesting as he found these new sounds and smells and sights, he missed the pet store. He'd loved the young owner, who used to carry him around so that he could see and sniff the other animals, or let him explore on the floor. She had played with him. At night, he had gone home with her.

Now that he lay quietly, he could just hear one of the new people shouting. He didn't trust them, with their shrill, strange voices. They didn't seem to like him. He'd come to a very interesting place, full of possibilities for hunting and playing, but he didn't think those two ladies were going to want to play with him.

He would hide for now and have a little nap. Later on, he could scout for food and water.

Maybe he could even find his way back to the pet store!

He fell asleep for awhile. When he woke up, he wanted to eat, but he heard pounding and shouting again and decided to stay hidden. The noises stopped and he jumped out of the slipper. But when he tried to leave the closet, he found its door pushed shut.

He ran to the strip of light and fresh air that came from under the door. He whined and then he barked.

No one came.

He sat and whined again, then whimpered.

He could feel a chilly draft blowing past his toes, toward the door. Air rushing into the back of the closet from somewhere, he realized. He caught a faint smell of mouse.

He knew about mice from the pet shop.

He sniffed around in the darkness and at last he found the old hole in the back of the closet. He dug at the spoiled, chewed edge of the carpet and pulled it back a bit more, away from the hole, and the draft became stronger.

Teacup put his head through the hole and barked several times. His voice got lost in the space between the walls.

He began to shove himself through the

hole with his back legs. The hole got tighter and tighter. He had a moment of panic when he seemed to be completely stuck, but a big last effort pushed him through into the space between two walls. Another hole, larger, let him through.

Now he found himself in another dark, strange place. Far to one side, he could see a bit of light. He couldn't hear anything. He trotted toward the dim light and found himself in a long corridor.

All his senses on alert, Teacup moved toward an open door he could just make out down the corridor. He peered around the corner of the door.

Inside, a dark shape lay on the floor. A dark human shape, he could tell from the smell.

He recognized the smell as that of the old lady who had taken him from the pet shop. He crept toward her, wondering why her breathing sounded so odd. She lay still.

When she moaned, Teacup's instinct told him to help. He found her face and gave her a little lick on the cheek. She didn't move at all. He tried again, then barked in her face.

Nothing.

This worried him. He sat and looked at the old woman. Something was very wrong here. He should look for the other woman to come help.

He licked the old woman again and waited. When nothing happened, he barked again.

Something stirred above him. He growled in surprise.

Then he recognized the scent of another human in the room.

"Quiff! Quiff! Quiff! Quiff!"

CHAPTER 17

Emily Wakes Up

$\mathcal{E}$MILY lay in a deep, dark, warm well of sleep, dreaming nothing, fearing and hoping nothing. The day's anxiety and discomfort and exertions had worn her out completely.

When she began to hear an odd, sharp sound, she only tried to burrow deeper into this comfortable nothingness, and sleep cuddled her so protectively she did not remember where she was or why.

The sound went on, came closer, more insistent. Stop, said the tiny conscious part of her thought. Go away, go away.

But it did not go away, did not stop. Though now, she also heard a scratching sound, a tiny thumping against the side of the bed.

Gradually, as the noises penetrated her fuggy mind, she recognized, against her will, the deep anxiety they tried to convey.

Then they stopped—stopped long enough for her to take a sharp breath in, open her eyes, and sit up.

Awake.

Where was she? She felt stupid and confused, but she knew she could not lie down again.

Suddenly she heard again the odd little voice that had pried its way into her unconsciousness: "Quiff! Quiff!"

She looked down, over the side of the bed.

The little dog—surely, a dog!—realized she had seen and heard him and began to dance and jump. Amazed at his size, for a moment

Emily had a dizzying feeling that he—and the floor—were much farther away than they really were, but she blinked and restored her sense of proportion.

She pulled her legs out from under the covers and climbed out of the bed. The little dog danced backward. Emily sat carefully on the raised floor around the bed and held out her hand for the dog to sniff.

She held her breath as he approached. As she sat letting him sniff her, she began to remember how she had come to this place and time.

The dog finally licked her hand and jumped up onto it. "Oh!" Emily said, surprised. She drew him close to her. "Oh, I love you!" The dog's bright eyes met hers with that deep calm intensity that a dog's eyes have. "I love you," she said more softly, and put him near her face. He kissed her again.

"But—where did you come from? My grandmother never said anything about a dog! Are you lost too?"

Gently, she put the dog back on the floor and stood and stretched. As soon as she got to her feet, he began to dance away, barking and looking back at her. Clearly, he meant for her to follow him.

She walked around the foot of the bed and then around to the other side.

And then she screamed.

Someone lay on the floor!

For a minute the whole room turned even darker and seemed to tilt. She ran across the room, backed into a wall, and pressed her hands against her mouth.

CHAPTER *18*

Rose Flees

ROSE sank to a chair. She had begun to tremble. *What,* then? Where had the child gone? Where *could* she go?

Emily must have gone home!

Yes, that's it! she told herself, flooded with relief. Emily had gone home by herself, angry about being taken to day care on Christmas Eve. She knew where Rose kept the emergency key hidden.

Rose snatched the phone up and put it to

94

her ear. No dial tone. She clicked the hang-up switch several times and heard a distant, hollow tone. She dialed with shaking fingers her home number and heard, as if from the moon, a series of rings.

One ring. Two. Three.

"Answer, Emily!" Rose cried. "Pick up!"

Four . . .

Then the answering machine picked up. Rose shouted into the phone, "Emily! Emily, if you're there, pick up! Pick up NOW!"

She waited, listening with all her might through the noises on the line. Nothing.

She hung up, then picked up to dial 9-1-1. This time the line was completely dead. In her panic, she dialed anyway, shouting that she needed help, that her boss was sick, her granddaughter missing. "Help! Come quickly!" She started to shout the address, then realized that it was no use. She let the receiver drop to the floor.

Rose stumbled back to the door Mrs. Bigley had gone through and pounded on it, yelling with all her might, but nothing happened. Then she hurried back to the kitchen, scrawled a note, and propped it up on the table:

GONE HOME—
MY GRANDDAUGHTER
IS MISSING!

She rushed to the closet and pulled on her coat, buttoned it badly, stuffed her hat on her head, shoved her feet into her boots, snatched up her purse and gloves, and fled.

CHAPTER 19

The Body on the Floor

EMILY still couldn't think for fear, but the little dog ran to the slumped figure and jumped against it, barking, nipping its fingers and face. Emily watched in horror, sure that she had been sleeping by a dead person's body.

But where had it come from?

And whose was it?

Suddenly the body began to moan, a terrifying sound, but it meant the person on the floor hadn't died. Emily sagged with relief. She could see, now, the white hair of an old woman.

The dog, excited by a sign of life, began barking at Emily. When Emily still didn't come toward him, he went back to trying to revive the old woman.

Emily found her courage and crept nearer. Mrs. Bigley, she thought. It must be Mrs. Bigley! She tried to say the name, but her voice didn't work. She tried again, and croaked it out.

More moans and a sob came from the form on the floor. Emily hurried across the room. The little dog jumped and kissed her when she knelt. She put her hand on the old woman's arm, giving a little shake. "Mrs. Bigley! Mrs. Bigley!"

The woman moaned again but did not open her eyes.

Oh, if this is Mrs. Bigley, she can tell me where my grandmother is! Emily thought. Then she thought, Grandma! Grandma *must* be near. She stood up and shouted, "Grandma! Grandma Rose!"

The sound made the old woman's eyelids flutter. She gasped, painfully, and twisted on the floor.

A ping sounded against the marble floor. Emily knelt to look.

A key!

She gasped and reached out for it, but the little dog raced forward and picked it up in his mouth and ran away from her, toward the door.

"No, no!" Emily cried, running after him. "Bad dog! Give it here!" The dog growled and ran into the dark corridor.

Emily started to follow. She had to get that key!

Just then, the old woman groaned so sorrowfully and painfully that Emily had to stop. She went back to the bed and pulled off a pillow. She put it under the old woman's head, then she dragged off the comforter and tucked it all around the old woman, cushioning her as well as she could from the cold floor.

Mrs. Bigley's eyelids fluttered at her.

"I'm going for help!" she told the near-lifeless body. "I'll come back. I promise, I'll come back!"

She ran into the corridor after the dog.

The darkness in the corridor stretched away on both sides. Which way had he gone? She crouched down and called, "Here, doggy! Come here!"

Then, out of the gloom to her left, she saw the pup appear. He couldn't bark because he still held the key in his mouth, but he wagged his tail at her and then turned to go farther down the corridor. He looked back at her.

"Okay, I'm coming!" Emily called softly. "Good dog! Good dog!"

The dog twice let her nearly catch up before running on ahead. She could just make him out. The corridor turned once, but she knew she could find her way back—it didn't branch out into other hallways.

The dog stopped at last. Emily slowed down and approached him very carefully, speaking gently. "Good dog, good boy! Give me the key, now." Finally, she knelt a couple of feet from him, her open palm outstretched.

And then—oh, thank heaven—the dog came forward and dropped the key into her hand.

Emily sprang up. "Oh, thank you! Thank you!"

She looked around in the murky hallway. "But where is the door?"

The little dog barked now and ran ahead a little way. Then he stopped and whined.

Emily caught up and felt the wall with her hand. A door! She found a keyhole and fumbled with the key for an agonizing minute before she got it fitted into the lock.

The key turned; the door swung open.

CHAPTER *20*

Where Is Grandma Rose?

EMILY stepped into a room so bright it dazzled her eyes. She had to cover them as she shouted, "Grandma! Grandma!"

No one answered. She peeked through her fingers as her eyes adjusted.

Then she dropped her arms and turned around and around in astonishment.

Nothing Grandma Rose had told her could have prepared her for the sight of all these doll-sized treasures. She gazed in awe.

Where is the doll? she wondered. Where is Grandma Rose?

What's happened here?

Throughout the space, she could see overturned and broken pieces of furniture, tangled linens, scattered tiny objects.

Had tiny thieves broken in?

"Grandma?" she called in a quieter voice. Would she find her grandmother tied up somewhere in this place? Was she, Emily, in danger? Emily froze and listened.

The little dog appeared again, in front of her. "Quiff! Quiff!" he barked.

This gave her courage. He's not afraid, she thought.

She strode forward, calling, "Grandma! Grandma Rose!" until she came to a regular-sized kitchen.

And there she saw something that gave her enormous hope. A teapot and a cup and saucer sat out on the table, exactly as they did at home when her grandmother made herself a cup of tea. Emily ran to the table. Yes! The same kind of teabags as at home!

She reached out and felt the pot, then yanked her hand back. Still hot! Very hot!

The tea had to be freshly made.

So—where was Grandma Rose?

Emily's eyes lit on the note propped on the table.

GONE HOME—
MY GRANDDAUGHTER
IS MISSING!

Oh no!

NO!

She couldn't believe it! Grandma Rose was out looking for *her*.

Emily raced to a window. She could barely see, through whirling snow, a road twisting away, far below, through dark fir trees.

And what else was there? She strained her

eyes and wiped away the steam she had made on the window.

A tiny moving figure, a blurred red shape, hurried against the wind, away from the house.

Emily pounded and pounded on the window. "Grandma! Grandma! Grandma!"

She knew that her grandmother could not hear her. She knew she should try to run after her, but she could not, after this long, dreadful, strange day, take her eyes off the one person in the world she loved. "Oh, Grandma!" she sobbed at last, pressing against the window. "Oh, Grandma Rose—I'm so sorry! I love you! Come back!"

CHAPTER 21

Out in the Cold

ROSE could not remember cold like this. Her winter things seemed so flimsy. Could Emily be out in this, somewhere? She prayed not. She tried to stay calm. One foot in front of the other, down the long drive.

She would find Emily and then send help for Mrs. Bigley.

Maybe she would see a police car when she got to the road!

She imagined the police car delivering her to her little house, where Emily's dear face would be watching through the window for her.

But what if Emily hadn't gone home?

She needed to think, but she couldn't stop to figure it out. She had to get help.

Images from the morning crowded her mind. Saying good-bye to Emily. Mrs. Bigley coming home with that little dog . . .

The dog!

Rose stopped just before entering the avenue of fir trees. She had forgotten all about the little dog.

She turned to look back at the house. She'd have to remember to tell the police about the dog.

She gazed up at the kitchen window.

CHAPTER 22

Emily's Bright Idea

EMILY stared with anguish through her tears. Even if she could find her way out of the house, she would never catch up with Grandma Rose.

Her grandmother continued to move away from the house.

Then, just before the curve in the road that would have taken her out of Emily's sight, the figure stopped and slowly turned.

And looked up.

Emily froze, then began to jump up and down and yell as loudly as she could. "It's me! Come back!"

The figure stared at the window. Emily jumped and waved her arms.

Her grandmother didn't seem to understand. She stood peering up, then turned and looked down the drive as if she wanted to continue on her way.

At last Grandma Rose looked up again. Emily had an idea. She ran to the light switch and began turning it off and on, off and on. Over and over.

She hated not being able to see her grandmother, but she had to go on signaling.

When she stopped and ran at last to the window, the figure had disappeared.

Had Grandma Rose vanished into the forest?

Or had she reached the outer door of the house, where Emily couldn't see?

Emily ran to the outer door, when suddenly

it pushed open against her, and her grand-mother, clothes crusted with snow, took her into her arms.

"Grandma, I love you, I love you, I love you!"

"Oh, darling! How on earth did you get here? Here, let me get these things off, I'll freeze you to death! Oh, Emily! You fright-ened me out of my wits!"

Emily helped Rose take off her coat and they threw themselves again into each other's arms.

Now Emily began to cry and could not stop. Rose gently led her, holding her tightly, into the kitchen and sat her down in a chair. She poured Emily some water. "Hush now, darling. It's all right, it's all right! We're together, that's all that matters . . . Here, drink this, sweetheart, have a good drink. . . . "

Emily sobbed some more before she could drink. Rose stood against the wall, looking at her, while she finished. Then she sat down. Emily grabbed her hands.

"Tell me, Emily. Tell me. You didn't go into Mrs. Debbs's?"

Emily, who could not yet talk, shook her head. She started to cry again, but Rose pressed her hands and said, "I understand, honey! It's all right!" She thought a moment. "You must have followed me. Then, when I got inside the house, you couldn't make me hear you?"

Emily nodded.

"But you did get in somehow. . . . Never mind! You can tell me about it later."

Just then, she heard, "Quiff! Quiff!" behind her. Rose gasped and turned around. "You! I keep forgetting all about you!"

Teacup trotted across the kitchen and took a long drink of water and then ate some kibble. Emily and Rose watched him. "Grandma Rose, you didn't tell me about the dog!"

"Mrs. Bigley only bought him today, honey. I didn't know he existed before."

"*Oh!*" Emily jumped up. "Mrs. Bigley!

Grandma, we have to go to her—she's . . . I thought she was dead, but she was moaning. . . . Oh, hurry!"

Emily ran through the rooms to the locked door, Rose and Teacup following. When she reached it, she panicked. "The key!"

She shoved her hands into her pockets and—relief!—pulled the key out of the right one. She handed it to Rose.

"Where on earth did you—" Rose started. Then she grabbed the key and opened the door.

Teacup and Emily ran ahead into the darkness.

At last, all three stepped into the beautiful bedroom and stared at the figure lying on the floor.

CHAPTER 23

The Strangest Christmas

EMILY woke up on the floor outside Mrs. Bigley's kitchen. For a moment she was confused, then, next to her, she felt movement and heard a slight murmur from her grandmother. Oh, yes, she thought. I remember now.

As quietly as she could, she began separating herself from the blankets and coats they'd made into a bed the night before. She had to go to the bathroom.

When she came back, she remembered the little dog. She pushed the kitchen door open and stepped inside, letting the door swing shut behind her. The storm had passed, and the window let in enough moonlight for her to see the little box on the floor. Then she heard, "Quiff! Quiff!"

Emily giggled and knelt by the box. "Are you okay?" she whispered. "Did you stay warm enough?" He felt wonderfully cozy when she lifted him up and set him on the floor. She sat in a kitchen chair while he ran to his dishes and took a long drink and some bites of kibble.

Emily saw her grandmother's desperate note, still on the table. It brought back all the terrors and wonders of the previous day. She shuddered to think how much danger she had put herself and her grandmother in. Tears welled in her eyes as she thought of her stubbornness and ungratefulness to Grandma Rose.

And poor Mrs. Bigley! She could have died of the shock of seeing Emily in that bed.

She should check on Mrs. Bigley for her exhausted grandmother, who had gotten up and down all night to see to the old woman. Emily picked up the dog and left the kitchen, threading through the darkened aisles between the dolls' furniture.

She still felt frightened of the old woman. She thought she would never forget the horror of waking up to see Mrs. Bigley stretched out on the floor. Or the fear she had felt when she and her grandmother had found her still unconscious. Memories flooded back.

Grandma Rose had exclaimed and rushed to Mrs. Bigley's side. She felt the old woman's pulse and put her head down to listen to her breathe. "She's alive! Did you cover her up like this?"

Emily nodded, limp with relief. Still alive!

"Good girl! Maybe she won't catch pneumonia. Is there water in there?" Rose pointed to the bathroom.

"Yes."

"Get me some in a glass if there is one, and bring a cloth. And you—shoo!" Teacup backed away from her.

Emily raced into the bathroom. She filled the crystal tumbler she'd seen earlier and pulled a washcloth from a swan's-head-shaped hook. In one corner it had elaborately embroidered initials: DLB. *D* for *Delilah*? she wondered. But this is a *real* little girl's room, I'm sure of that!

"Wake up, ma'am! Everything's all right. I'm here!" Rose wet the cloth in the tumbler and wiped Mrs. Bigley's face. Then she let some drops fall on her forehead. The old woman's eyes fluttered.

Rose looked up at Emily. "Don't let her see you!" she mouthed. Emily went to the other side of the bed and sat down on the floor. The dog jumped into her lap.

"Come on, Mrs. Bigley. Wake up, now. We've got to get you out of this cold place."

"Ohhh. Oh, Rose! Where—"

"Shhh, take it easy. You had a fall. Can you move everything all right?"

Emily listened to the faint sounds of movement. Then Rose said, "Oh, good! Nothing's broken, thank heaven!"

"Rose, I have to tell you—"

"No, don't try to talk. Let's just get you safe and warm and then—"

"No! Please, Rose—listen!"

"Tell me, then."

The old woman's voice dropped to a harsh whisper. "She's here!"

"Oh! You remember her. Well, let me explain—"

"Rose, she's really here! My Delilah, my little girl—she's back! Alive! I saw her!"

Silence. Emily held her breath. What did the poor old lady mean?

Then Rose spoke gently. "Was this your daughter's room?"

"Yes. And when I came in, I saw her! In the bed!"

"No, no you di—"

"*Yes!* Oh, if only I had known! She *couldn't* come back until the doll died. I thought"— Mrs. Bigley sobbed—"I thought, I'll keep the doll just the way my Delilah would have wanted her, I'll play with her just like she would have. But that was wrong!"

"Mrs. Bigley . . . "

"It was because of that doll, that terrible doll, that my darling girl died! You didn't know that, did you? She was my mother's doll, and I wanted to play with her my whole childhood. But I wasn't allowed even to touch her. And I promised myself I'd let *my* child play with her, if I ever had one. And I had a little girl, at last, when I was grown up. I even named her after the doll I'd wanted so much to hold. But by then I knew how valuable the doll was, and I kept saying, no, not until you're older, not yet. Oh! Oh! Oh!" Mrs. Bigley began to cry.

"There, now," Rose comforted. "You were right to take care. It's not a suitable doll for a child, anyone would do the same. . . . "

Mrs. Bigley choked out, "Rose, I killed my child! I put the doll up high, where she couldn't reach her. But she could see her. And when I was out of the room . . . she climbed up! And the whole shelf fell down on her!"

"Oh, ma'am! Oh, I'm so sorry!"

"But the doll! The doll wasn't even scratched! She was sitting on the floor with her eyes open, looking at me. Blaming me."

"No, no. . . . It was an accident."

"My fault."

"So you kept the doll. To punish yourself."

"Yes. If she had been played with, it wouldn't have happened. But, Rose! Help me get up! Look, look in the bed—she's back! She's forgiven me—I suffered long enough, and all I needed to get my girl back was for that doll to die . . . "

"Listen to me!" Rose spoke fiercely. "It was *not* your daughter in the bed. It was my granddaughter. You must understand this! Emily, come here!"

Emily stood up, cradling the dog in her

arms. She walked around the bed and stood at Mrs. Bigley's feet.

Mrs. Bigley stared up at her.

"This is my granddaughter, Emily. My son's little girl, who came to live with me when he and his wife died. She has something to say to you."

Emily had trouble starting her story, but once she started, the words tumbled out, the whole miserable, frightening day. Finally she finished. "I'm really really really sorry!" she exclaimed. "And I'll pay for the window, I will!"

Mrs. Bigley said nothing for a long time. She lay with her eyes closed. Rose continued to rub her hands. Emily sank down to the floor, and the dog jumped from her arms. All of them watched Mrs. Bigley.

She spoke at last without opening her eyes. "Your son died, Rose?"

"Yes, ma'am. Emily's father. And her mother."

"I remember now. But—I didn't even notice, really! How wicked!" Mrs. Bigley began to cry.

And, before Rose or Emily could stop him,

the dog leaped across Mrs. Bigley's legs, ran up to her face, and kissed it.

The old woman's wet eyes flew open and she turned her head. "Oh! I'd forgotten—"

Teacup had broken the spell of silence in the room. "Never you mind, ma'am," Rose said quickly. "Let's get you standing up now."

Together, Emily and Rose had helped Mrs. Bigley back to her warm bedroom and gotten her into her bed. They'd helped her eat some soup, taken some themselves, put the little dog into his box with his blanket tucked around him, and then, at last, made their own bed and dropped to sleep at once, too tired even to talk.

Now, Emily crept into Mrs. Bigley's room and made sure the old woman's covers hadn't come off. She could hear her snoring faintly. She took Teacup—she had finally learned his name—back into the doll's house and began at last, by the first pink light of dawn, to examine all the treasures she'd set out to see so long, long, long ago.

And then she remembered. "Merry Christmas!" she whispered to Teacup, settling down in front of the tiny tree. She found the switch for its lights and turned them on. "Merry Christmas!"

CHAPTER 24

Nearly One Year Later

EMILY squirmed on her school bus seat. Next to her, her best friend, Jennifer, said, "We're almost there!"

Two girls in the seat ahead turned around. "Emily, you are *so* lucky!" one said.

A boy across the aisle said, "Yeah, lucky to go on a field trip. I can't believe we're going to see a *doll*!" But he seemed nearly as excited as the girls.

The bus turned right between two pillars,

then drove along a curving drive between great stands of fir trees. Emily looked at them in the bright early winter light. They looked so ordinary compared to last Christmas Eve.

The bus pulled into a new parking lot, and the class climbed out. Over heavy glass doors set into the front of the Bigley mansion, a banner proclaimed:

OPENING TODAY

THE DELILAH L. BIGLEY MUSEUM

FOR CHILDREN

EXHIBITION:

THE DELILAH COLLECTION

Emily stared up at the house. So much had happened in the past year!

Her teacher called, "Emily, please lead us into the new museum."

Up the steps they went, through the glass doors. The lady at the desk stood up and said,

"Oh, hello! Our very first visitors! Emily, you know the way."

Emily led everyone down a corridor to the right. At the end of it, over an open arch, a sign read:

DELILAH'S TREASURE HOUSE

They entered what had once been a ball-room, Emily now knew. And there stood Grandma Rose! Emily ran to her.

"Welcome, Ms. Waters's class," Grandma Rose said. "I am Mrs. Rose Miller, the curator of this collection. That means I'm the person who takes care of things in a museum. In this position, I am continuing the work I began several years ago, when this was the home of Mrs. Jane Bigley. Mrs. Bigley inherited Delilah, the doll you will see who inspired the collection, and she personally selected almost everything you'll see today. I say 'almost all,' because, since work began on the museum, people from around the world have donated items to the exhibit.

"Now, please come this way. We will begin with Delilah's living room."

Delilah's furnishings had been set up on a waist-high platform laid out like the floorplan of a house. Each "room" had clear plastic walls, low enough for children to look through, on which hung moldings that framed spaces where windows and doors would be in a real house. Visitors could walk around the entire house and see everything from as many angles as possible. The whole exhibit had been decorated for Christmas.

The children distributed themselves around the doll-sized living room. It took Rose quite some time before she could get them to quit pointing, nudging, and squealing at the scene. She pointed out the more important pieces, and told them about her work cataloging and arranging the exhibit.

They went over each room in this way. The museum had hooked the house to water and electricity, so Rose could demonstrate that the lamps, sinks, stove, bathtub, and even the toilet really worked.

"And now, I have a special surprise for you. Mrs. Jane Bigley herself has come to the museum today to greet you."

Mrs. Bigley rolled into the exhibit in a wheelchair pushed by an attendant. She took Rose's hand, and Rose gave her a hug.

"Thank you for coming today, children," Mrs. Bigley said. "Mrs. Miller has done an excellent job. Let's give her a big hand!"

Everyone applauded, Emily hardest of all.

"Now, do you have questions for me?"

Jennifer raised her hand. "Where is the doll?"

"Ah, I expected someone would ask. Mrs. Miller?"

Rose disappeared, returning quickly with Delilah, dressed magnificently in a silk gown. Everyone gasped.

"What happened to her face?" someone asked.

"She fell last Christmas Eve," Mrs. Bigley answered. "I have decided *not* to have her fixed. One trouble with being a collector is that you tend to become a perfectionist. That is never healthy. Keeping Delilah like this reminds me of that. And I wish I had known it much earlier. Now, if you would please put Delilah into her house, Mrs. Miller?"

Grandma Rose unlatched one of the side panels and swung it out. Then she placed Delilah on her chaise longue. She pulled a shawl around the doll's shoulders and opened a tiny book, which she put into Delilah's hands. The girls all said, "Ah . . . " The boys rolled their eyes. Grandma Rose shut the case.

Some other children had questions, which Mrs. Bigley and Emily's grandmother answered. Finally, the children were allowed to explore on their own. Emily ran to Mrs. Bigley.

"How are you today, ma'am?" she asked.

"Oh, Emily. I'm just fine, but I'm so glad I have this chair now. I'm not getting any younger! I see that you are blooming. And how is that rascal, Teacup?"

"He's fine. He's still growing. The vet says it's because he's happy."

"Good. I'm glad he's not staying so *very* tiny. It wasn't safe for him."

"He's still pretty small. I'll bring him to visit you soon."

"Please do! Now, you go join your friends, young lady."

"Thank you!" Emily started toward Jennifer, but she turned, ran back, and hugged Mrs. Bigley again. "Thank you again for Teacup. And for everything!"

Mrs. Bigley held her. "Emily, it is you who should be thanked. If you hadn't come—"

"I shouldn't have!"

"I know. But you did. And we're both much better for it."

"I'll see you on Christmas, Mrs. Bigley."

"Yes, Christmas! The happiest Christmas ever!"